Alligator Pie & Other Poems

A DENNIS LEE TREASURY

A Dennis Lee Treasury

ALLIGATOR PIE
& other poems

HarperCollins*Publishers*Ltd

For Kevyn, Hilary, and Julian,
and for Sacha and Jade

HarperCollins books may be purchased for educational, business
or sales promotional use through our Special Markets Department.

HarperCollins Publishers Ltd
Bay Adelaide Centre, East Tower
22 Adelaide Street West, 41st Floor
Toronto, Ontario, Canada
M5H 4E3

www.harpercollins.ca

Library and Archives Canada Cataloguing in Publication
Title: Alligator pie : and other poems / a Dennis Lee treasury.
Other titles: Poems. Selections (2020)
Names: Lee, Dennis, 1939- author. | Newfeld, Frank, 1928- illustrator. | Wijngaard, Juan,
illustrator. | McPhail, David, 1940- illustrator. | container of (work): Lee, Dennis, 1939-
Alligator pie. | container of (work): Lee, Dennis, 1939- Jelly Belly.
container of (work): Lee, Dennis, 1939- Ice cream store.
Description: Illustrations by Frank Newfeld, Juan Wijngaard, and David McPhail.
Identifiers: Canadiana 20200214241 | ISBN 9781443411691 (hardcover)
Classification: LCC PS8523.E3 A6 2020 | DDC jC811/.54—dc23

Printed and bound in Italy

RTL 9 8 7 6 5 4 3 2 1

Contents

ALLIGATOR PIE

the poems were written by DENNIS LEE
the pictures were drawn by FRANK NEWFELD

Alligator Pie

Alligator pie, alligator pie,
If I don't get some I think I'm gonna die.
Give away the green grass, give away the sky,
But don't give away my alligator pie.

Alligator stew, alligator stew,
If I don't get some I don't know what I'll do.
Give away my furry hat, give away my shoe,
But don't give away my alligator stew.

Alligator soup, alligator soup,
If I don't get some I think I'm gonna droop.
Give away my hockey-stick, give away my hoop,
But don't give away my alligator soup.

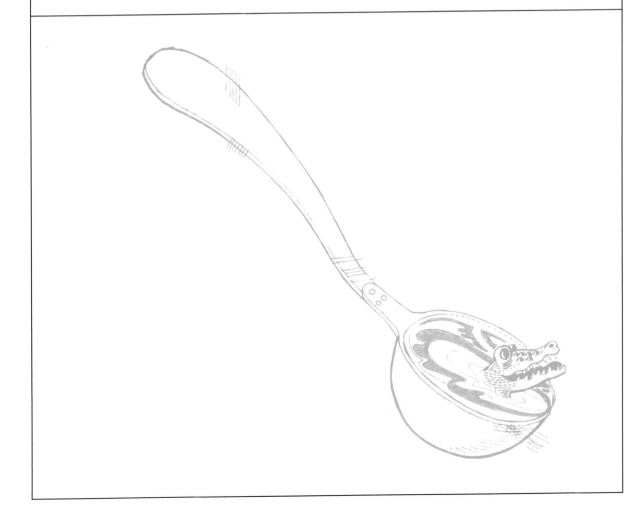

Wiggle to the Laundromat

Wiggle to the laundromat,
Waggle to the sea;
Skip to Casa Loma
And you can't catch me!

Singa Songa

Singa songa sea
I've got you by the knee.

Singa songa sand
I've got you by the hand.

Singa songa snail
I've got you by the tail.

Singa songa seat
And it's time to eat!

Bouncing Song

Hambone, jawbone, mulligatawney stew,

Pork chop, lamb chop, cold homebrew.

Licorice sticks and popsicles, ice cream pie:

Strawberry, chocolate, *vanilla!!!*

5

Street Song

Sidewalk,
Hippity hop,
Step on a crack
Or you can't come back.

Skippity one,
Skippity two,
Wait for the mailman
And kick off your shoe.

Mumbo, Jumbo

Mumbo   Jumbo
Christopher Colombo
I'm sitting on the sidewalk
Chewing bubble gumbo.

I think I'll catch a WHALE . . .
I think I'll catch a *snail* . . .
I think I'll sit around awhile
Twiddling my thumbo.

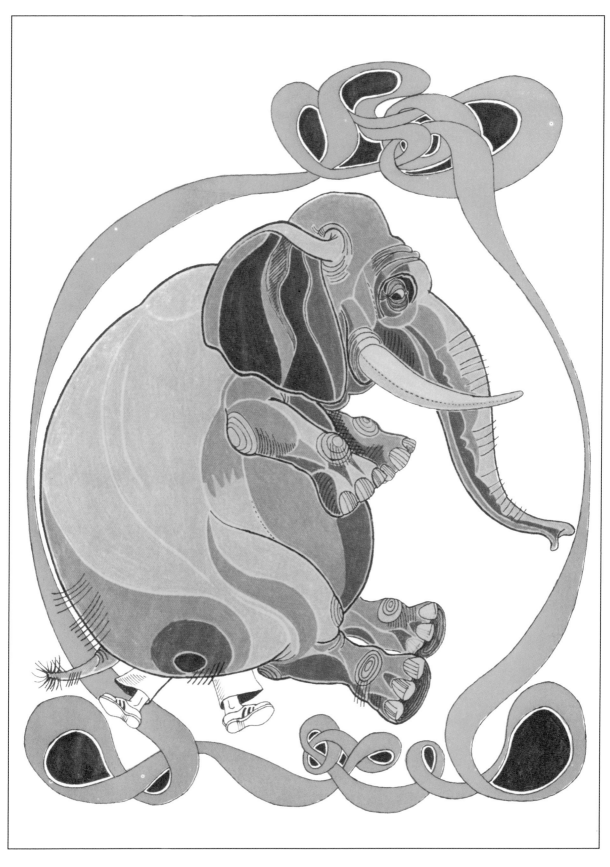

Willoughby Wallaby Woo

Willoughby, wallaby, woo.
I don't know what to do.

Willoughby, wallaby, wee.
An elephant sat on me.

Willoughby, wallaby, wash.
I'm feeling kind of squash.

Willoughby, wallaby, woo.
And I don't know what to do.

Lying on Things

After it snows
I go and lie on things.

I lie on my back
And make snow-angel wings.

I lie on my front
And powder-puff my nose.

I *always* lie on things
Right after it snows.

Rattlesnake Skipping Song

Mississauga rattlesnakes
Eat brown bread.
Mississauga rattlesnakes
Fall down dead.
If you catch a caterpillar
Feed him apple-juice;
But if you catch a rattlesnake
Turn him loose!

Bed Song

Yonge Street, Bloor Street,
Queen Street, King:
Catch an itchy monkey
With a piece of string.

Eaton's, and Simpson's,
And Honest Ed's:
Give him his pyjama pants
And throw him into beds!

In Kamloops

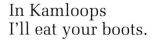

In Kamloops
I'll eat your boots.

In the Gatineaus
I'll eat your toes.

In Napanee
I'll eat your knee.

In Winnipeg
I'll eat your leg.

In Charlottetown
I'll eat your gown.

In Crysler's Farm
I'll eat your arm.

In Aklavik
I'll eat your neck.

In Red Deer
I'll eat your ear.

In Trois Rivières
I'll eat your hair.

In Kitimat
I'll eat your hat.

And I'll eat your nose
And I'll eat your toes
In Medicine Hat and
    Moose Jaw.

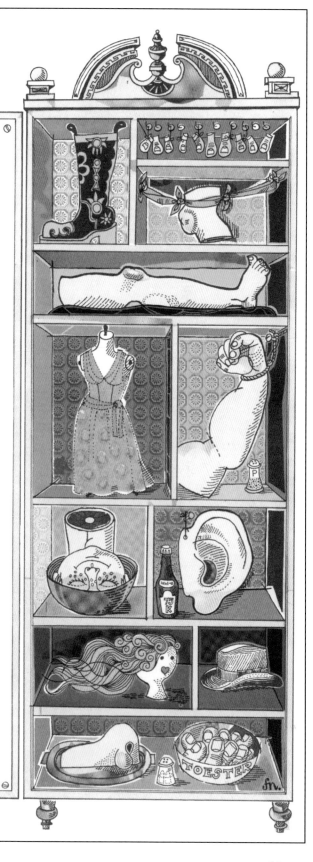

Billy Batter

Billy Batter,
What's the matter?
How come you're so sad?
   I lost my cat
   In the laundromat,
And a dragon ran off with my dad,
   My dad—
A dragon ran off with my dad!

Billy Batter,
What's the matter?
How come you're so glum?
   I ripped my jeans
   On the coke machine,
And a monster ran off with my mum,
   My mum—
A monster ran off with my mum!

Billy Batter,
Now you're better—
Happy as a tack!
    The dragon's gone
    To Saskatchewan;
    The monster fell
    In a wishing-well;
    The cat showed up
    With a new-born pup;
    I fixed the rips
    With potato chips,
And my dad and my mum came back,
    Came back—
My dad and my mum came back!

Ookpik

An Ookpik is nothing but hair.
If you shave him, he isn't there.

He's never locked in the zoo.
He lives in a warm igloo.

He can whistle and dance on the walls.
He can dance on Niagara Falls.

He has nothing at all on his mind.
If you scratch him, he wags his behind.

He dances from morning to night.
Then he blinks. That turns out the light.

Bump on Your Thumb

Who shall be king of the little kids' swing?
Jimmy's the king of the little kids' swing
With a bump on your thumb
And a thump on your bum
And tickle my tum in Toronto.

Who shall see stars on the climbing bars?
Jimmy sees stars on the climbing bars
With a bump on your thumb
And a thump on your bum
And tickle my tum in Toronto.

And who shall come home with the night for his throne?
Jimmy's come home with the night for his throne
With a bump on your thumb
And a thump on your bum
And tickle my tum in Toronto.

I'm stuck

newfeld

Flying Out of Holes

Mr Mole. Mr Mole! MR MOLE!!!
Come quick. I'm stuck in a hole.

Burrow along with your snout.
I'm stuck and I can't get out.

Push me and pull me. I'll pop
Straight up in the air, kerplop!

Aren't you going to come,
You no-good burrowing bum?

Never mind. I'm growing wings
To fly out of holes and things.

Now I'm flying straight up in the air.
When you get here, I'll land on your hair.

I flew right out of that hole.
Goodbye! Goodbye, Mr Mole.

William Lyon Mackenzie King

William Lyon Mackenzie King
Sat in the middle & played with string
And he loved his mother like *any*thing—
William Lyon Mackenzie King.

Tony Baloney

Tony Baloney is fibbing again—
Look at him wiggle and try to pretend.
Tony Baloney is telling a lie:
Phony old Tony Baloney, goodbye!

Skyscraper

Skyscraper, skyscraper,
Scrape me some sky:
Tickle the sun
While the stars go by.

Tickle the stars
While the sun's climbing high,
Then skyscraper, skyscraper
Scrape me some sky.

Tricking

When they bring me a plate
Full of stuff that I hate,
Like spinach and turnips and guck,
I sit very straight
And I look at the plate
And I quietly say to it: "YUCK!"

Little kids bawl
'Cause I used to be small,
And I threw it all over the tray.
But now I am three
And I'm much more like me—
I yuck till they take it away.

But sometimes my dad
Gets ter*riff*ickly mad,
And he says, "Don't you drink from that cup!"
But he can't say it right
'Cause he's not very bright—
So I trick him and drink it all up!

Then he gets up and roars;
He stomps on the floor
And he hollers, "I warn you, don't eat!!"
He counts up to ten
And I trick him again:
I practically finish the meat.

Then I start on the guck
And my daddy goes "Yuck!"
And he scrunches his eyes till they hurt.
So I shovel it in
And he grins a big grin.
And then we have dessert.

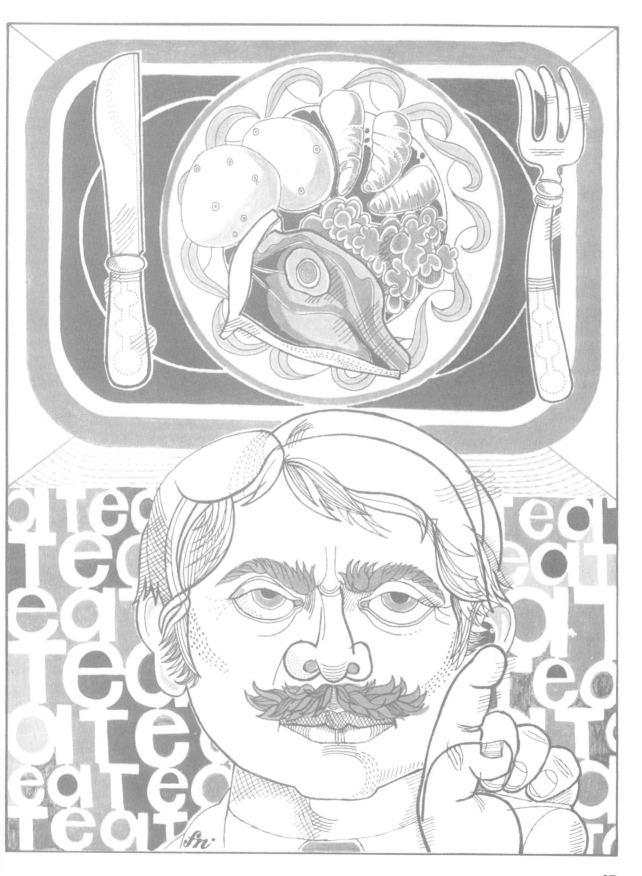

27

I Found a Silver Dollar

I found a silver dollar,
But I had to pay the rent.
I found an alligator,
But his steering-wheel was bent.
I found a little monkey,
So I took him to the zoo.
Then I found a sticky kiss and so
I brought it home to you.

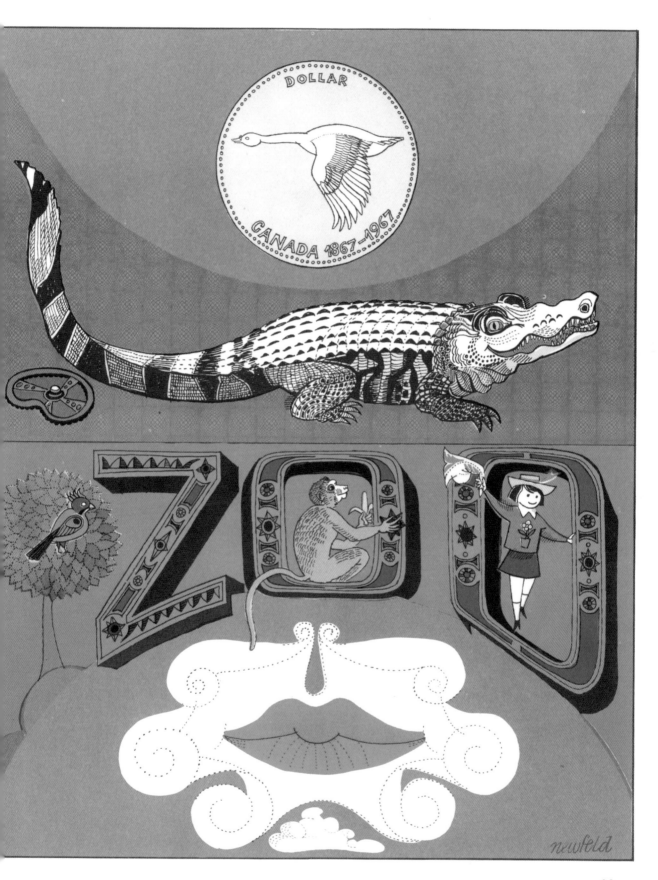

newfeld

29

If You Should Meet

If you should meet a grundiboob,
Comfort him with sugar cubes.
Then send him on his way again
With feather beds, in case of rain.

If you meet him going out
Place a doughnut on his snout.
But if you meet him coming back,
Give his nose a mighty whack.

And if you meet a potamus,
Sleeping on a cotamus,
Do not sing or talkamus,
But take him for a walkamus.

If you should meet a crankabeast,
Be sure his forehead isn't creased;
Then pat him gently on his heads
And tuck him quickly into beds.

Higgledy Piggledy

Higgledy piggledy
Wiggledy wump,
I met a man
Who caught a mump:
With his left cheek lumpy
And his right cheek bumpy—
Higgledy piggledy
Wiggledy wump.

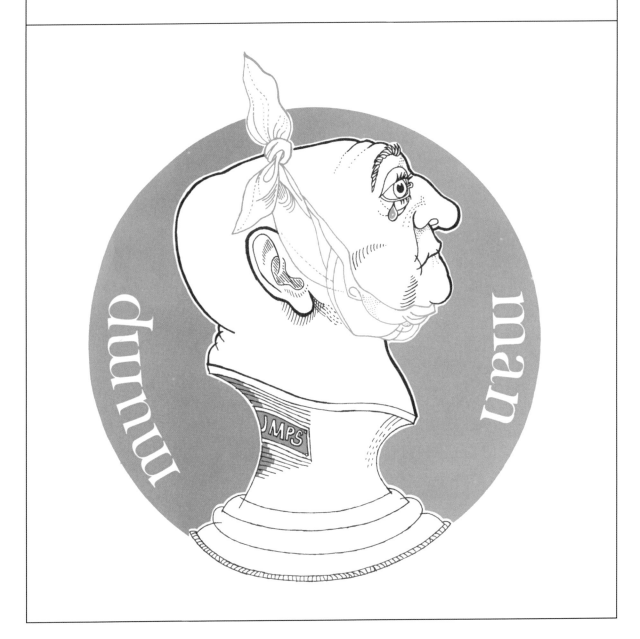

Higgledy piggledy
Sniggledy sneezle,
I met a man
Who caught a measle:
With his chest all dots
And his face all spots—
Higgledy piggledy
Sniggledy sneezle.

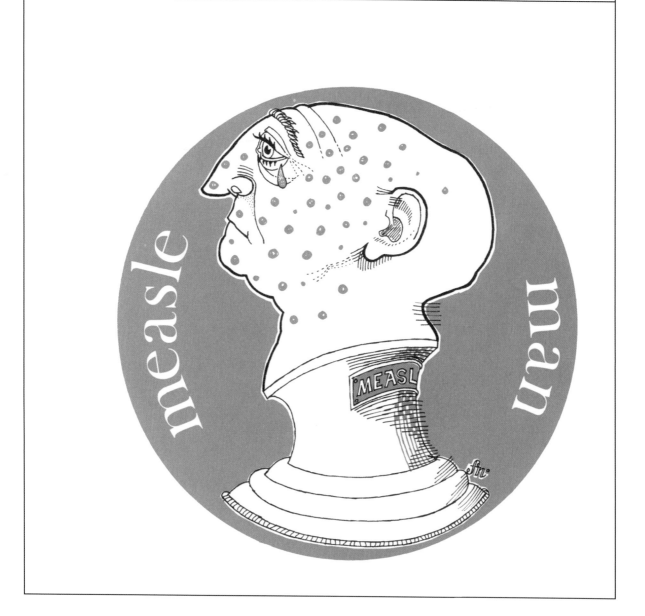

Thinking in Bed

I'm thinking in bed,
'Cause I can't get out
Till I learn how to think
What I'm thinking about;
What I'm thinking about
Is a person to be—
A sort of a person
Who feels like me.

I might still be Alice,
Excepting I'm not.
And Snoopy is super,
But not when it's hot;
I couldn't be Piglet,
I don't think I'm Pooh,
I know I'm not Daddy
And I can't be you.

My breakfast is waiting.
My clothes are all out,
But *what* was that thing
I was thinking about?
I'll never get up
If I lie here all day;
But I still haven't thought,
So I'll just have to stay.

If I was a Grinch
I expect I would know.
I might have been Batman,
But I don't think so.
There's so many people
I don't seem to be—
I guess I'll just have to
Get up and be me.

Nicholas Grouch

Nicholas Grouch
Has filled his pouch
With garbage lids and bears.
When he gets home
His wife will groan
And throw him down the stairs.

more

Nicholas Grouch
Has filled his pouch
With wet potato peelings.
When he gets back
His wife will yack
And hang him up on the ceiling.

Nicholas Grouch
Has filled his pouch
With licorice sticks and toffee.
When he gets in
His wife will grin
And give him a cup of coffee.

Psychapoo

Psychapoo,
The silly goose,
Brushed his teeth
With apple-juice.

Psychapoo,
The melon-head,
Rode his bicycle
In bed.

His mother said,
"Sit down and eat!"
He swallowed the plate
And left the meat.

His father asked him,
"Can't you hear?"
He had a carrot
In his ear.

He met a dog
And shook its tail,
Took a bath
And caught a whale,

Put it in his
Piggy bank,
Said, "I think I'll
Call it Frank."

His brother asked him,
"Can't you see?"
He drank his hair
And combed his tea.

He took a trip
To Newfoundland,
Walking on water
And swimming on land

And every time
He heard a shout,
He took his pencil
And rubbed it out.

It isn't me,
It isn't you,
It's nutty, mutty
Psychapoo.

On Tuesdays I Polish My Uncle

I went to play in the park.
I didn't get home until dark.
But when I got back I had ants in my pants
And my father was feeding the shark.

I went to play in the park,
And I didn't come home until dark.
And when I got back I had ants in my pants
And dirt in my shirt, and glue in my shoe,
And my father was tickling the shark.

I went to sleep in the park.
The shark was starting to bark.
And when I woke up I had ants in my pants,
Dirt in my shirt, glue in my shoe,
And beans in my jeans and a bee on my knee,
And the shark was tickling my father.

My father went off to the park.
I stayed home and read to the shark.
And when he got back he had ants in his pants,
Dirt in his shirt, glue in his shoe,
Beans in his jeans, a bee on his knee,
Beer in his ear and a bear in his hair,
So we put him outside in the ark.

I started the ark in the dark.
My father was parking the shark.
And when we got home we had ants in our pants,
Dirt in our shirt, glue in our shoe,
Beans in our jeans, a bee on our knee,
Beer in our ear and a bear in our hair,
A stinger in our finger, a stain in our brain,
And our belly buttons shone in the dark.

So my dad he got snarky and barked at the shark
Who was parking the ark on the mark in the dark.
And when they got back they had ants in their pants,
Dirt in their shirt, glue in their shoe,
Beans in their jeans, a bee on their knee,
Beer in their ear and a bear in their hair,
A stinger in each finger, a stain in the brain,
A small polka-dot burp, with headache tablets,
And a ship on the lip and a horse, of course,
So we all took a bath in the same tub and went to bed early.

The Fishes of Kempenfelt Bay

Under the bubbles
Of Kempenfelt Bay,
The slippery fishes
Dawdle all day.

They park in the shallows
And wiggle and stray,
The slippery fishes
Of Kempenfelt Bay.

I ride on a bike.
I swing in the gym.
But I'd leave them behind
If I knew how to swim

With the slippery fishes
That dawdle all day,
Under the bubbles
Of Kempenfelt Bay.

Kahshe or Chicoutimi

If I lived in Temagami,
Temiskaming, Kenagami,
Or Lynx, or Michipicoten Sound,
I wouldn't stir the whole year round

Unless I went to spend the day
At Bawk, or Nottawasaga Bay,
Or Missinabi, Moosonee,
Or Kahshe or Chicoutimi.

Tongue Twister

Someday I'll go to Winnipeg
To win a peg-leg pig.
But will a peg-leg winner win
The piglet's ill-got wig?

Someday I'll go to Ottawa
To eat a wall-eyed eel.
But ought a wall-eyed eater
Pot an eel that isn't peeled?

Someday I'll go to Nipigon
To nip a goony loon.
But will a goony nipper lose
His loony nipping spoon?

The Hockey Game

(With thanks to A.A. Milne)

Squirm
Was a
Worm
With a Terrible
Temper.
Wee
Was a flea
With a Big Bad Roar.
X
Was an elephant
Who couldn't keep his
Laces tied.
And **George** was a bit of a bore.

Squirm played
Hockey with a
Great big
Tooth-pick.
Wee played
Hockey with her
Friends and her foes.
X played
Hockey but he
Couldn't keep his
Laces tied.
And **George** just played with his toes.

Squirm threw a
Bodycheck and
Sent **X**
Flying.
Wee shot the
Puck and she
Knocked **X** flat.

X cried
Tears that were
Bigger than piano stools.
And **George** floated round in a hat.

Now
Squirm
Is a worm
With a Very
Soggy Temper.
And **Wee**
Is a flea
With a Waterlogged Roar.
X is an
Elephant who
Wonders where his
Skates went.
And **George** is rather wet
　　George is *very* wet
　　George is Awful wet
　　　　　　　　　　once
　　　　　　　　　　　more.

Peter Rabbit

Peter Rabbit's
Mother sighed,
"Son, you'd better
Stay inside."

Peter Rabbit's
Father said,
"Don't you dare
Get out of bed!

"For if you do
You'll sneak away
And like a shot
You'll go and play

"In Farmer J.
MacGregor's garden—
Planning, without
A beg-your-pardon,

"To bolt his luscious
Turnips down
While we are shopping
In the town."

Peter yawned
At this to-do.
"So what?" he asked.
"You eat them too."

"It's not at all
The same," they said,
From either side
Of his messy bed,

"For since you will not
Use your spoon,
You'll turn into
A Spotted Goon!"

thank you, Miss Beatrix

"Shut up, dear parents,"
Peter cried,
"You know I'd never
Sneak outside

"And wolf those luscious
Turnips down,
While you are shopping
In the town!"

Then Peter hummed
A loving hum,
And watched his tired old
Dad and mum

Teetering out
And tottering down
The steep steep hill
To the shops in town.

Then up he sprang
And off he sped
With visions of turnips
Alive in his head;

And up he rose
And off he ran
To where the turnip
Patch began.

He pulled up one.
He pulled up two.
He stuffed them in
And gave a chew.

And down they went
Kerplunk, because—
He crammed them in
With just his paws!

Then woe betide us!
Lack-a-day!
Good gosh, gadzooks and
Wellaway!

Quick, thick and fast
In inky blots
His fur broke out
With horrid spots.

He raced inside
To find a mirror;
The awful change
Grew clear and clearer:

Without a doubt
He was a Goon—
Because he *would* not
Use a spoon!

 Is this the end
Of Peter's tale?
A Goon-like life
In a spotted jail?

No, no! Again
I say it—No!
Great heavens! Let it
Not be so!

For thinking of
His dreadful doom
He cried, "I Should Have
Used A Spoon!"

And pondering
His piteous plight
He roared, "My Dad
And Mum Were Right!"

At once his face
Began to shine.
He lit up like
A neon sign

Till someone put him
On T.V.
And parents forced
Their kids to see

The Shiny Spotted
Goody-Goon,
Who *Never* Ate
Without a Spoon.

Well, that's the story.
Here's the moral:
'Hare today
And Goon tomorrow.'

The Friends

When Egg and I sit down to tea
He never eats as much as me.
And so, to help him out, I take
A double share of chocolate cake.
And when we get a special treat
He says he really couldn't eat—
Not even fudge, or licorice loops
Or butterscotch caramel ice-cream soup.
And likewise, if the juice is fine,
He always whispers, "Please drink mine."
And since Egg is my special friend
I gulp it down to the bitter end.
And Eggy says, when I hug him tight,
"I'm glad I had an appetite."

When Egg and I go out to play
His legs are always in the way,
And so he seems to fall a lot
And always in a muddy spot.
And since Egg is my special friend
I fall down too; and I pretend
To cover myself with guck and dirt
So Eggy's feelings won't be hurt.
And when my mother starts to frown
I 'splain that Egg kept falling down,
And she throws us both in the washing machine,
And Eggy says, "I'm glad you're clean."

And when we go to bed at night
He sort of hates to shut the light.
He mentions, in a little voice,
"I hear a burglar kind of noise."
And also, "Giants scare me most."
And also, "That looks like a ghost!"
And since Egg is my special friend
I say that ghosts are half pretend.

I tell him everything's all right,
And I hide in the covers with all my might,
And then I get up and turn on the light.
And when the room is friends again
We snuggle down, like bears in a den,
Or hibernating in a cave.
And Eggy says, "I'm glad we're brave."

The Sitter and the Butter and the Better Batter Fritter

My little sister's sitter
Got a cutter from the baker,
And she baked a little fritter
From a pat of bitter butter.
First she bought a butter beater
Just to beat the butter better,
And she beat the bit of butter
    With the beater that she bought.

Then she cut the bit of butter
With the little butter cutter,
And she baked the beaten butter
In a beaten butter baker.
But the butter was too bitter
And she couldn't eat the fritter
So she set it by the cutter
    And the beater that she bought.

And I guess it must have taught her
Not to use such bitter butter,
For she bought a bit of batter
That was sweeter than the butter.
And she cut the sweeter batter
With the cutter, and she beat her
Sweeter batter with a sweeter batter
    Beater that she bought.

Then she baked a batter fritter
That was better than the butter
And she ate the better batter fritter
    Just like that.

But while the better batter
Fritter sat inside the sitter—
Why, the little bitter fritter
Made of bitter butter bit her,
Bit my little sister's sitter
    Till she simply disappeared.

Then my sister came to meet her
But she couldn't see the sitter—
She just saw the bitter butter
Fritter that had gone and et her;
So she ate the butter fritter
    With a teaspoonful of jam.

Now my sister has a bitter
Butter fritter sitting in her,
And a sitter in the bitter
Butter fritter, since it ate her,
And a better batter fritter
Sitting in the silly sitter
In the bitter butter fritter
    Sitting in my sister's tum.

Windshield Wipers

Windshield wipers
Wipe away the rain,
Please bring the sunshine
Back again.

Windshield wipers
Clean our car,
The fields are green
And we're travelling far.

My father's coat is warm.
My mother's lap is deep.
Windshield wipers,
Carry me to sleep.

And when I wake,
The sun will be
A golden home
Surrounding me;

But if that rain
Gets worse instead,
I want to sleep
Till I'm in my bed.

Windshield wipers
Wipe away the rain,
Please bring the sunshine
Back again.

Hockey-sticks and High-rise: A Postlude

When I started reading nursery rhymes to my children, I quickly developed a twitch. All we seemed to read about were little pigs and kings. The details of *Mother Goose*—the pipers and piemen and pence—had become exotic; children still loved them, but they were no longer home ground.

Not that this was a bad thing. But I started to wonder: shouldn't a child also discover the imagination playing on things she lived with every day? Not abolishing Mother Goose, but letting her take up residence among hockey-sticks and high-rise too? I began experimenting.

I started with the nursery rhymes in the first part of this book. And one thing I discovered is that the words should never be sacred. A rhyme is meant to be used, and that means changing it again and again. For children's verse passes around in weird and wonderful versions, and the changes always make sense—to the tongue and the ear, if not always to the mind. If your child rewrites some of these poems, please take his version as seriously as mine.

By the same token, you should feel free to relocate the place-poems. Put in the streets and towns you know best; the rhythm and rhyme may get jostled a bit, but so what?

I also discovered that nursery rhymes can't be approached at an adult's reading rate. They unfold much more slowly. In fact, they need to be brought to life almost as tiny plays, preferably with much pulling of faces and bouncing of rear-ends on knees. One of these four-line poems may take a couple of minutes to complete, especially if you drop in new words and verses.

I had never realized how soon a child can take part in "doing poems." A two-year-old will join in, if you pause at the rhyme-word and let her complete it. Usually it will be the familiar rhyme, but if you're making up new verses you'll be surprised by what she thinks of. Try starting a verse "Alligator steak," or "Willoughby wallaby wungry."

I hope the main thing I learned is invisible. There is a class of poem whose sole virtue is that it Contains a Worthy Sentiment, or Deals With the Child's Real World. Adults sometimes tolerate these wretched exercises, thinking they must be Literature. Young children, I can report, don't.

For I did commit a few of these pious versicles. They were awful, of course; wherever a poem comes from, it's not from good intentions. The undisguised boredom of my listeners persuaded me to pitch them out. And eventually I realized that the hockey-sticks and high-rise would find their own way into the poem, without orders from me. Which is when it really got to be fun.

DL, 1974

How Do You Illustrate
Poems That Don't Need Pictures?

What could (or should) illustration contribute, when the poetry, as written, is complete unto itself, as is invariably the case with Dennis Lee's books? The artwork might have an explanatory function if the poetry needed fortification, but surely not where the author's voice is loud and clear. Of course, the obvious reason might be "to dress up the package" in an attractive manner, the pictures acting the role of a candy wrapper. But there must be better reasons for incorporating, or even needing, a visual component.

Merely translating the poet's creation word for word into a visual tongue may bore, rather than engage, the young reader. An illustration can gently side-step the poet and perhaps stimulate a youthful imagination with its interpretation of the poem. It may even leave the young viewer to avow: "That's interesting, but *my* poet has said other things too, and I can draw lots more and way better pictures!"

There can be magic between author and reader in the poetry book for children. Illustration may enhance the magic, and might well inspire a reader to re-envisage the poem in the poet's footsteps. It could even motivate some of our young people to conjure up their own "flights-of-fancy" and artistry! This is as true in today's computer age as it was when *Alligator Pie* was first published.

FN, 2012

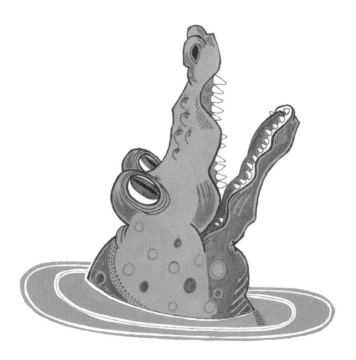

JELLY BELLY

Dennis Lee

Illustrated by Juan Wijngaard

The Dreadful Doings of Jelly Belly

Jelly Belly bit
    With a big fat bite.
Jelly Belly fought
    With a big fat fight.

Jelly Belly scowled
    With a big fat frown.
Jelly Belly yelled
    Till his house fell down.

Liza Briggs

Lazy lousy Liza Briggs
Wouldn't get up to feed the pigs.
The pigs pulled off the comforter
And jumped right into bed with her.

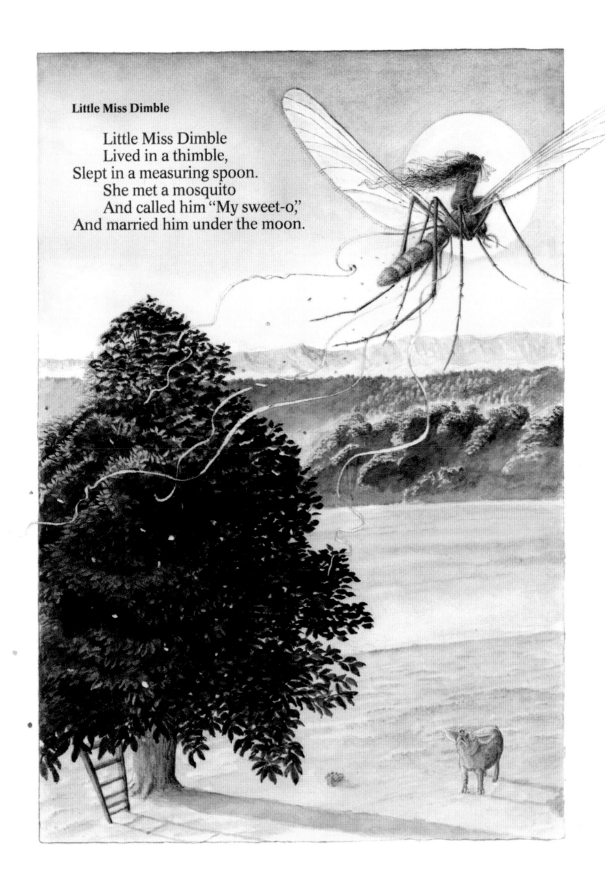

Little Miss Dimble

Little Miss Dimble
Lived in a thimble,
Slept in a measuring spoon.
She met a mosquito
And called him "My sweet-o,"
And married him under the moon.

Hugh, Hugh

Hugh, Hugh,
At the age of two,
Built his house in a big brown shoe.
Hugh, Hugh,
What'll you do?
There's holes in the soles
And the rain comes through!

Mrs Magee

Mrs Magee
Climbed into a tree,
And she only came down to go shopping.
A branch was her bed,
With a leaf on her head—
And whenever it rained, she got sopping.

69

There Was an Old Lady

There was an old lady
    Whose kitchen was bare,
So she called for the cat
    Saying, "Time for some air!"

She sent him to buy her
    A packet of cheese.
But the cat hurried back
    With a basket of bees.

She sent him to buy her
    A gallon of juice.
But the cat reappeared
    With a galloping goose.

She sent him to buy her
    a blueberry snack.
But the cat scampered home
    With a cute lumberjack.

She sent him to buy her
    A bowl of ice cream.
But the cat skated in
    With a whole hockey team.

She sent him to buy her
    A bite of spaghetti.
But the cat strutted up
    With a bride and confetti.

She sent him to buy her
    A fine cup of tea.
But the cat waddled back
    With a dinosaur's knee.

The fridge was soon bulging,
    And so was the shelf.
So she went for a hot dog
    And ate it herself.

Kitty-cat, Kitty-cat

Kitty-cat,
Kitty-cat,
Will you be mine?
I'll bring you
Milk and I'll
Make your coat shine.

You'll be my
Puss, and you'll
Sleep in my bed—
Under the
Coverlet,
Right by my head.

72

The Garbage Men

What a lucky
    Bit of luck—
The garbage men
    In the garbage truck!

One has a can, and
    One has a pan, and
One is a big fat
    Canadian!

Easy, Peasy

Easy, peasy, paperboy,
Patch your coat with corduroy,
Marching like a soldier boy,
    Bringing us the paper.

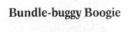

Bundle-buggy Boogie

Well, way up north
On a fine bright day,
A bundle-buggy boogied
At the break of day.

It did the boogie-woogie here,
It did the boogie-woogie there,
It did the bundle-buggy boogie-woogie
Ev-er-y-where:

    Calabogie,
    Kapuskasing,
    Espanola,
    Atikokan;
    Manitoulin,
    Madawaska,
    Mindemoya,
    Moosonee!

Then another bundle-buggy
Did a boogie-woogie hop,
And another and another
In the bundle-boogie bop.

And it's boogie-woogie high,
And it's boogie-woogie low,
And it's bundle-buggy boogie-woogie
Everywhere you go:

    Athabasca,
    Abitibi,
    Bona Vista,
    Malaspina;
    Bella Bella,
    Bella Coola,
    Batchawana,
    Baie Comeau!

No

No, no, no!
They're always saying no.
Is nothing ever good enough
But no, no, no?

Dickery Dean

"What's the matter
     With Dickery Dean?
He jumped right into
     The washing machine!"

"Nothing's the matter
     With Dickery Dean—
He dove in dirty,
     And he jumped out clean!"

Dawdle, Dawdle, Dawdle

Dawdle, dawdle, dawdle,
It's the uncles and the aunts,
Dawdling with their shoes and socks,
Dawdling with their pants.
    So hurry up
    And scurry up
    And hurry, scurry, worry up—
Thank goodness there are kids around
To make them stop their dawdling.

Dawdle, dawdle, dawdle,
It's the daddies and the mums,
Dawdling with their apple-juice,
Dawdling with their crumbs.
    So hurry up
    And scurry up
    And hurry, scurry, worry up—
Thank *goodness* there are kids around
To make them stop their dawdling!

Three Tickles

Pizza, pickle,
Pumpernickel,
My little guy
Shall have a tickle:

One for his nose,
And one for his toes,
And one for his tummy
Where the hot dog goes.

Doodle-y-doo

Doodle-y-doo,
Doodle-y-doo:
I lost my baby,
And what shall I do?

Doodle-y-dee,
Doodle-y-dee:
Open my fingers
And what do I see?

A baby!

Counting Out

One for coffee
One for tea
And one to run
To Calgary.

The Army Went A-marching

Oh the army went a-marching
    And they marched across the tum;
Round and round the tummy with a
    Mighty army drum.

And it's first toe,
    Second toe,
    Third toe, and
    Four;
Tickle the top of the fifth toe—
    And then you march some more.

Oh the army went a-hopping
    And they hopped across the snout;
Round and round the sneezer with a
    Mighty army shout.

And it's first toe,
    Second toe,
    Third toe, and
    Four;
Tickle the tip of the fifth toe—
    And then you hop some more.

Boogie Tricks

One, two, three:
The cat ran up the tree.

Four, five, six:
He did some boogie tricks.

Seven, eight, nine:
He boogied on the line.

Ten, eleven, twelve:
He boogied by himself.

Chicoutimi Town

Which is the way to Chicoutimi town?
Left foot up, and right foot down.
Right foot up and left foot down,
That is the way to Chicoutimi town.

The Kitty Ran Up the Tree

The kitty ran up the tree,
The kitty ran up the tree,
    Her nose went up
    And her toes went up
And the kitty ran up the tree.

Why did she climb the tree?
To see what a kitty could see.
    But all she could see
    At the top of the tree
Was the tip of the top of the tree—

       So—

The kitty came down the tree,
The kitty came down the tree,
    Her nose came down
    And her toes came down
And the kitty came down the tree.

Five fat fleas
Upon a trapeze
Did somersaults one by one.
A flea flew, a flea flew,
A flea flew, a flea flew,
A flea flew, and then there were none.

Four fat frogs
On tumbledown logs
Did somersaults one by one.
A frog flew, a frog flew,
A frog flew, a frog flew,
(Clap), and then there were none.

Three fat cats
On calico mats
Did somersaults one by one.
A cat flew, a cat flew,
A cat flew, *(clap)*,
(Clap), and then there were none.

Two fat ants
In dancing pants
Did somersaults one by one.
An ant flew, an ant flew,
(Clap), *(clap)*,
(Clap), and then there were none.

One fat bee
On a billygoat's knee
Did somersaults one by one.
A bee flew, *(clap)*,
(Clap), *(clap)*,
(Clap), and then there were none.

No fat gnomes
On a dinosaur's bones
Did somersaults none by none.
(Clap), *(clap)*,
(Clap), *(clap)*,
(Clap), and then there were none.

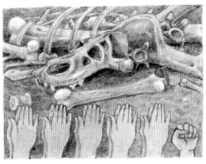
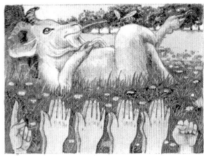

One fat bee
On a billygoat's knee
Did somersaults one by one.
A bee flew, *(clap)*,
(Clap), *(clap)*,
(Clap), and then there were none.

Two fat ants
(Etcetera, ad nauseam).

The Seven Kinds of Bees

Now, there are seven kinds of bees:
Bees that buzz, and bees that tease,
Bees that tickle, bees with fleas,
And bees with burrs upon their knees,
Bees that shyly murmur Please—
And bees that nip your nose off!

The Puzzle

Annie and Ernie
    McGilligan Spock
Pedalled their tricycles
    Round the block.

They pedalled and pedalled
    And pedalled in pairs,
Till they came to a house
    That was just like theirs.

In the same front yard
    Stood the same small tree;
On the same brown table
    The same pot of tea;

And the very same smells!
    And the very same noise!
And the very same beds
    With the very same toys!

They stood and they stared
    And they stared and they stood;
The thing was too weird
    To be understood:

How was it possible?
    Think of the shock
Of Annie and Ernie
    McGilligan Spock!

Can You Canoe?

Can you canoe
In Kalamazoo?
Can you canoe
In Kamloops?
Can you canoe
At a quarter to two
In a van when the traffic
Jam loops?

I *can* canoe
In Kalamazoo;
I *can* canoe
In Kamloops;
But I cannot canoe
At a quarter to two
In a van when the traffic
Jam loops.

(Canoe?)

Freddy

Here is the story
Of Freddy, my friend,
Who ran out in traffic—
And that is the end.

Skit, Scat

Skit, scat,
Scaredy-cat:
Scoot, skedaddle
And don't come back!

Catching

The boys catch the girls
And the girls catch the boys:
Kissing in the schoolyard,
What a yucky noise!

Meet Me

Meet me at the parking lot,
Meet me in the ditch,
Meet me at the corner
With the seven year itch!

Spaghetti-o!

Oh-oh, spaghetti-o:
Eat it with confetti-o.
When it's ready, let it go!

Hey, Man

Hey, man,
Cool, man—
You're a silly
Fool, man.

Double-barrelled Ding-dong-bat

Why,
You—

Double-barrelled,
Disconnected,
Supersonic
Ding-dong-bat:

Don't you dare come
Near me, or I'll
Disconnect you
Just like that!

Dirty Georgie

Georgie's face was
Never clean,
Georgie smelled like
Gasoline.

Kissing Georgie—
Mighty fine!
Just like kissing
Frankenstein!

Georgie, Georgie,
Wash your face,
Or we'll kick you out
Of the human race:

Not because you're ugly,
Not because you're cute,
Just because your dirty ears
Smell like rubber boots!

News of the Day

Neighbour, neighbour, tell me do:
What's the news at noon?

Believe it or not, an astronaut
Is walking on the moon.

Jenny Shall Ride

Jenny shall ride in a carriage,
Jenny shall ride on a sleigh.
And I'll be the king of tomorrow,
And she shall be queen of today.

The Maple Tree

My maple tree
Is neat to climb,
And there's a special
Branch of mine

Where I can perch
And not be seen,
And watch the world
Go by, and dream.

Shoo, Doggie, Shoo!

Shoo, doggie, shoo!
I'm not in love with you.
    You like to fight,
    And your teeth might bite,
So shoo, doggie, shoo!

Mr Lister's Dog

Mr Lister lost his dog,
And Mrs Lister found him,
And Sister Lister fetched him home
And tied a ribbon round him.

Carey Cut

Carey cut the back yard,
Carey cut the front;
Carey cut the house in two—
What a silly stunt!

Over and Over

Over and
   Over,
Come over
   To me:
I'll be your
   Friend if
You want me
   To be.

Cookies and
   Juice, at
A quarter
   To three:
Over and
   Over,
Come over
   To me.

Under the Garden Hose

Dinkelpuss, and Twinkletoes,
And Chuck-Me-Under-the-Chin,
All ran under the garden hose
To see if they could swim.

The water felt so hot,
The water felt so cold,
The water felt like soda pop
And now my tale is told.

Knock! Knock!

Knock! Knock!
    Who's there?
Captain Cook
    In his underwear.

Knock! Knock!
    Who's that?
Jacques Cartier
    In a tall silk hat.

Doctor, Doctor

Doctor, Doctor, fix my head:
I'm feeling sick and I'll soon be dead!

Little girl, little girl, drink some juice:
You think too much and your brain's come loose.

Doctor, Doctor, here's a dime:
You saved my life for the forty-second time.

Sailing to Sea

I'm sailing to sea in the bathroom,
    And I'm swimming to sea in a tub,
And the only song that I ever will sing
    Is rub-a-dub dub-a-dub dub.

A duck and a dog and a submarine
    Are sailing together with me,
And it's rub-a-dub-dub
And it's dub-a-dub-dub
    As we all sail out to sea.

The Voyage

The cowboy and the carpenter,
The collie and the cook,
Sailed the blue Pacific
On a telephone book.

They sailed for forty nights.
They sailed for forty days.
They gobbled tons of hot cross buns
With a dab of mayonnaise.

Rock Me Easy

(very slowly)

Rock me easy,
    Rock me slow,
And rock me where
    The robins go,

And rock the branch,
    And rock the bough,
And rock the baby
    Robins now,

And rock them up
    And rock them down
And rock them off
    To sleepy town,

And rock me slowly
    Up the stairs
To snuggle down
    With my teddy bears,

And rock me easy,
    Rock me slow,
And rock me where
    The robins go.

The Little Old Man

A little old man
Went up in space,
And he got ice cream
All over his face,

Sooo—

Wash him with a wash-cloth,
Roll him in a rug,
And tuck him in a blanket
Till he's snug, snug, snug!

The Bear and the Bees

Wiggle waggle went the bear,
Catching bees in his underwear.
One bee out,
And one bee in,
And one bee bit him
On his big bear skin.

The Tiny Perfect Mayor

A tiny perfect mayor
With a tum, tum, tum,
Tried to toddle round the block
To meet his mum, mum, mum.
He took a tiny tumble
On a crumb, crumb, crumb,
And he cried, "I wish I'd never
Ever come, come, come."

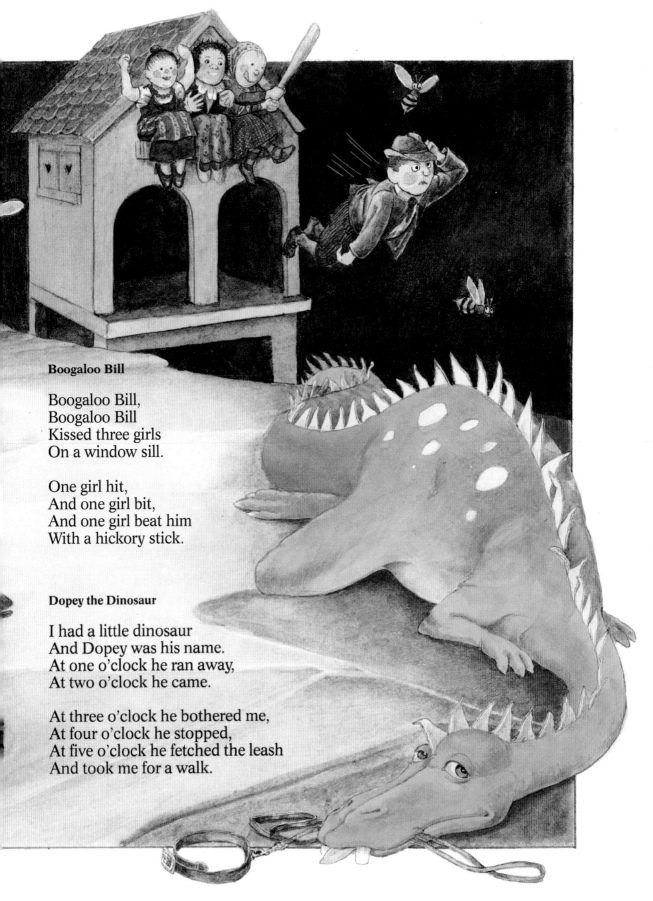

Boogaloo Bill

Boogaloo Bill,
Boogaloo Bill
Kissed three girls
On a window sill.

One girl hit,
And one girl bit,
And one girl beat him
With a hickory stick.

Dopey the Dinosaur

I had a little dinosaur
And Dopey was his name.
At one o'clock he ran away,
At two o'clock he came.

At three o'clock he bothered me,
At four o'clock he stopped,
At five o'clock he fetched the leash
And took me for a walk.

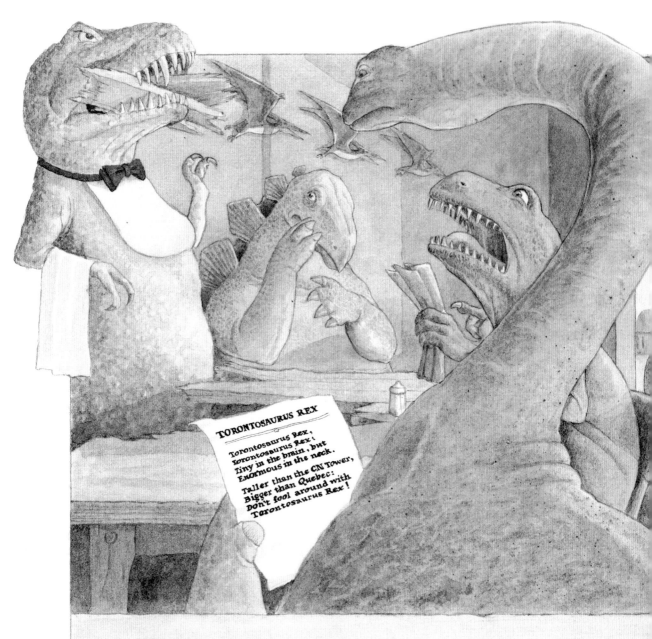

TORONTOSAURUS REX

Torontosaurus Rex,
Torontosaurus Rex!
Tiny in the brain, but
Enormous in the neck.

Taller than the CN Tower,
Bigger than Quebec:
Don't fool around with
Torontosaurus Rex!

The Dinosaur Dinner

Allosaurus, stegosaurus,
Brontosaurus too,
All went off for dinner at the
Dinosaur zoo;

Along came the waiter, called
Tyrannosaurus Rex,
Gobbled up the table
'Cause they wouldn't pay their checks.

Anna Banana

Anna Banana, jump into the stew:
Gravy and carrots are *good* for you.
 Good for your teeth,
 And your fingernails too,
So Anna Banana, jump into the stew!

Peter Stampeder

Peter Stampeder went out on his horse.
He wanted to capture a bad guy, of course.
The bad guy was busily robbing a train.
So Peter Stampeder came back home again

Robber J. Badguy

Robber J. Badguy
Was robbing a bank,
His manners were mean
And his underwear stank.

The neighbours got angry
As grizzly bears,
Bumped him and thumped him
And threw him downstairs.

William Lyon Mackenzie

William Lyon Mackenzie
Came to town in a frenzy—
    He shot off his gun
    And made himself run,
William Lyon Mackenzie.

Peterkin Pete

Poor little Peterkin Pete:
His family had nothing to eat.
    They looked in the cupboard
    And whimpered and blubbered,
Poor little Peterkin Pete.

Brave little Peterkin Pete:
His family had nothing to eat.
    He went to the Prairies
    And picked them some berries,
Brave little Peterkin Pete!

The Excellent Wedding of the Broom and the Mop

Hippity, lippity, lop!
The broom shall marry the mop.
    The puppy shall bow,
    The puss shall miaow,
And the piggy shall go for the pop,
    The pop—
The piggy shall go for the pop.

Hippity, lippity, lop!
The broom has married the mop.
    The pussy got up
    For a dance with the pup,
And the piggywig guzzled the pop,
    The pop—
The piggywig guzzled the pop.

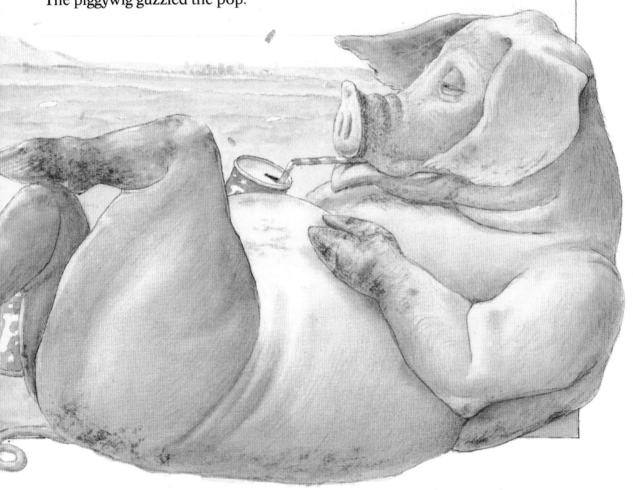

Mrs Murphy, and Mrs Murphy's Kids

Mrs Murphy,
    If you please,
Kept her kids
    In a can of peas.

The kids got bigger
    And the can filled up,
So she moved them into
    A measuring cup.

But the kids got bigger
    And the cup got crammed,
So she poured them into
    A frying pan.

But the kids grew bigger
    And the pan began to stink,
So she pitched them all
    In the kitchen sink.

But the kids kept growing
    And the sink went *kaplooey*,
So she dumped them on their ears
    In a crate of chop suey.

But the kids kept growing
    And the crate got stuck,
So she carted them away
    In a ten-ton truck.

And she said, "Thank goodness
    I remembered that truck,
Or my poor little children
    Would be out of luck!"

106

But the darn kids grew
    Till the truck wouldn't fit,
And she had to haul them off
    To a gravel pit.

But the kids kept growing
    Till the pit was too small,
So she bedded them down
    In a shopping mall.

But the kids grew enormous
    And the mall wouldn't do,
So she herded them together
    In an empty zoo.

But the kids grew gigantic
    And the fence went *pop!*
So she towed them away
    To a mountain top.

But the kids just grew
    And the mountain broke apart,
And she said, "Darned kids,
    They were pesky from the start!"

So she waited for a year,
    And she waited for another,
And the kids grew up
    And had babies like their mother.

And Mrs Murphy's kids—
    You can think what you please—
Kept all *their* kids
    In a can of peas.

My Doodle-bug Won't Come Home

My doodle-bug won't come home.
No, my doodle-bug won't come home.
   He likes to roam
   And he won't come home,
And my doodle-bug won't come home.

My doodle-bug climbed the wall.
Yes, my doodle-bug climbed the wall.
   I said he'd fall
   If he climbed a wall,
But my doodle-bug climbed the wall.

And my doodle-bug won't come home.
No, my doodle-bug won't come home.
   He likes to roam
   And he's *still* not home,
And my doodle-bug won't come home.

Pussy-willow

Pussy-willow,
    Pussy-willow,
Like a cater-
    Pillar's pillow—
Spring is near
    When you appear,
Pussy-willow
    Mine-o.

Granny Spider

Granny Spider
Sits and knits,
She sits and knits
With all her wits.
She spins a line
Of silky twine,
And sits and knits all day.

Little Mr Mousiekin

Little Mr Mousiekin
Sitting in your housiekin,
Eating bread and barley corn—
Little Mr Mousiekin.

Zinga, Zinga

Zinga, zinga, zumpkin:
A pussy on a pumpkin.
A puss in the light
But a witch at night!
Zinga, zinga, zumpkin.

The Ghost and Jenny Jemima

(slow and spooky)

The clock struck one,
The clock struck two,
The ghost came playing
Peekaboo.
    Wa-OOO!
    Wa-OOO!

The clock struck three,
The clock struck four,
And Jenny Jemima
Began to roar.
    Wa-OOO!
    Wa-OOO!

The clock struck five,
The clock struck six,
The ghost could walk through
Steel and bricks.
    Wa-OOO!
    Wa-OOO!

The clock struck seven,
The clock struck eight,
And Jenny Jemima's
Hair stood straight.
    Wa-OOO!
    Wa-OOO!

The clock struck nine,
The clock struck ten…
The ghost wound the clock,
And went home again.

THE END.

The Birthday Present

There was a little guy
With a twinkle in his eye,
And he hadn't any money
For to spend, spend, spend.

So he made a wooden flute
With a root-toot-toot,
And he played it at the party
For his friend, friend, friend.

Thumbelina

Thumbelina came to town,
Pigtails up and petticoats down,
All the children crowding round—
    Tiny Thumbelina!

Thumbelina, dance on my thumb,
Tap your toes with a rum-tum-tum!
Boys on piano, girls on drum—
    Play for Thumbelina!

Up in North Ontario

Up in North Ontario
A barber met a bear-io
And cut his curly hair-io,
Up in North Ontario.

Christmas Tree

Christmas tree,
    You're green as green,
The prettiest tree
    I've ever seen,

The shiniest tree
    I've ever known—
I'll dream about you
    When I'm grown.

The Snowstorm

Heave-ho,
Buckets of snow,
The giant is combing his beard.
The snow is as high
As the top of the sky,
And the world has disappeared.

Going, Going, Gone

Going, going, gone,
Your daddy won't be long.
Where did he go?
To shovel the snow.
Going, going, gone.

The Gentle Giant

Every night
At twelve o'clock,
The gentle giant
Takes a walk;
With a cry cried high
And a call called low,
The gentle giant
Walks below.

And as he walks,
He cries, he calls:

"Bad men, boogie men,
Bully men, shoo!
No one in the neighbourhood
Is scared of you.
The children are asleep,
And the parents are too:
Bad men, boogie men,
Bully men, shoo!"

Good Night, Good Night

The dark is dreaming.
Day is done.
Good night, good night
To everyone.

Good night to the birds,
And the fish in the sea,
Good night to the bears
And good night to me.

Silverly

Silverly,
    Silverly,
Over the
    Trees
The moon drifts
    By on a
Runaway
    Breeze.

Dozily,
    Dozily,
Deep in her
    Bed,
A little girl
    Dreams with the
Moon in her
    Head.

The Ice Cream Store

poems by
Dennis Lee

pictures by
David McPhail

THE ICE CREAM STORE

Oh, the kids around the block are like an
    Ice cream store,
'Cause there's chocolate, and vanilla,
    And there's maple and there's more,

And there's butterscotch and orange—
    Yes, there's flavours by the score;
And the kids around the block are like an
    Ice cream store!

COPS AND ROBBERS

Up and down the fire escape,
Round and round the alley,
   The cops ran up,
   The robbers ran down—
"STOP!" said Mrs O'Malley.

GREEN FOR GO

It's red for STOP,
And green for GO—
And catch him all over
Ontario!

SKIPPING (OLGA)

My girl friend's name is Olga,
She's from the River Volga.
She can skip, she can vault, she can somersault—
My acrobatic Olga.

STINKY

My boy friend's name is Stinky,
He comes from cold Helsinki.
He's four foot two, and he smells like glue—
My dinky, slinky Stinky.

DIGGING A HOLE TO AUSTRALIA

We're digging a hole to Australia,
    But it's going kind of slow.
And we've got some juice and cookies,
    But they're getting kind of low.

And there's lots of kids in Australia,
    So we brought a sandwich to share;
But if this hole doesn't hurry,
    The sandwich will never get there . . .

We're digging a hole to Australia,
    Or else to Timbuctoo—
I hope those kids know we're coming,
    And they make us a snack or two!

THE PERFECT PETS

WAL— *I had a DOG,*
    And his name was Doogie,
    And I don't know why
    But he liked to boogie;

    He boogied all night
    He boogied all day
    He boogied in a rude
    Rambunctious way.

SO— *I got a CAT,*
    And her name was Bing,
    And I don't know why
    But she liked to sing;

    She sang up high
    She sang down deep
    She sang like the dickens
    When I tried to sleep.

SO— *I got a FOX,*
    And her name was Knox,
    And I don't know why
    But she liked to box;

    She boxed me out
    She boxed me in
    She boxed me *smack!*
    On my chinny-chin-chin.

SO— *I got a GRIZZLY,*
    And his name was Gus,
    And I don't know why
    But he liked to fuss;

    He fussed in the sun
    He fussed in the rain
    He fussed till he drove me
    Half insane!

NOW— *I don't KNOW,*
    But I've been told
    That some people's pets
    Are good as gold.

    But there's Doogie and there's Bing,
    And there's Knox and Gus,
    And they boogie and they sing
    And they box and they fuss;

    So I'm giving them away
    And I'm giving them for free—
    If you want a perfect pet,
    Just call on me.

FREE Pets

NINE BLACK CATS

As I went up
To Halifax,
I met a man
With nine black cats.

ONE was tubby,
TWO was thin,
THREE had a pimple
On his chin-chin-chin;

FOUR ate pizza,
FIVE ate lox,
SIX ate the wool
From her long black socks;

SEVEN had a dory,
EIGHT had a car,
And NINE sang a song
On a steel guitar.

So tell me true
When you hear these facts—
How many were going
To Halifax?

THE DANGEROUS TALE OF THE DINOSAURUS DISHES

Oh, the mumosaurus washed,
    And the dadosaurus dried,
And the kidosaurus took them
    In her wagon for a ride.

"STOP!" cried the dadosaurus,
    "STOP!" cried the mum,
And, "STOP!" cried the lady
    Who was chewing bubble gum.

MAXIE AND THE TAXI

Maxie drove a taxi
With a *beep! beep! beep!*

And he picked up all the people
In a heap, heap, heap.

He took them to the farm
To see the sheep, sheep, sheep—

Then, Maxie and the taxi
Went to sleep, sleep, sleep.

MABEL

Mabel dear
It's not a stable:
Take your front legs
Off the table,

Place your hooves
Upon the floor,
And do not whinny
Any more.

WAITER, DEAR WAITER

Waiter, dear waiter, please come on the run;
Bring me a cheeseburger baked in a bun.

Customer, customer, what can I do?
A mouse stole the cheese, and the hamburger too.

If there's no burger, then bring me the bun.
If there's no bun, then my dinner is done.

HERMAN THE HOOFER

Herman was a hoofer.
  He hoofed the night away.
He did a fancy two-step
  On the streets of Mandalay.

He tripped the light fantastic
  Down by blue Montego Bay.
Then Herman hid his hoofing shoes
  And slept the livelong day.

COOL PILLOW

Pillow, cool pillow,
Come snuggle with me,
Drift me to sleep
Where I'm longing to be;

Birds in the nest
And the nest in the tree—
So pillow, cool pillow,
Come snuggle with me.

THE VISIT

Saturday night
The moon was bright,
And the Martians began to sing;
And the leader came down
In a calico gown,
Demanding to see the King.

The King was away
Till the end of May.
The Queen had a very bad back.
So the Peppermint Prince
With a packet of mints
Invited them in for a snack.

Saturday night
The moon was bright,
And the Martians began to dance.
Oh, the party was gay
As they gamboled away
In their brand-new calico pants.

WE THANK YOU! they cried
As they gamboled outside,
Where the lawn was alight with dew.
(*We thank you!* they whispered
In calico slippers,
As into the darkness they flew . . .)

Saturday night
The moon was bright,
And the Martians had flown away.
So the Queen and the Prince
Had the rest of the mints,
And the King came home in May.

A WONDERFUL TRIP IN A ROCKETSHIP

It isn't far to where you are,
    Not if you know the way:
Just zoom around the planet earth—
    It takes about a day.

Nantucket, Pawtucket, Biloxi, and Boise,
Manhattan, Milwaukee, and Maine,
Rocketing by in the blink of an eye—
Yosemite, Yonkers, Spokane.

See how the world spins round and round,
    Like since the world began;
And look—two kids and a spotty dog
    Are racing in Pakistan!

Uruguay, Paraguay, Pampas, La Paz,
Panama City, Peru;
Haiti, Havana, and Copacabana—
Quito, Quintana Roo.

And what do they eat in Bangladesh?
    What do they drink in Rome?
Do kids play tag, or hide and seek,
    In London, Linz, and Nome?

Zambia, Gambia, Zongo, the Congo,
Passing like shooting stars—
Maputo and Mali, Zimbabwe, Malawi,
Zambezi and Zanzibar.

So many faces, so many places,
    So many people to see:
But look, my friend—we're home again,
    And now
            it's time
                for tea.

CHILLYBONES

Chillybones, chillybones—
Who's got the chillybones?

Rub them, and scrub them,
And warm up their sillybones!

THE SECRET PLACE

There's a place I go, inside myself,
  Where nobody else can be, .
And none of my friends can tell it's there—
  Nobody knows but me.

It's hard to explain the way it feels,
  Or even where I go.
It isn't a place in time or space,
  But once I'm there, I *know*.

It's tiny, it's shiny, it can't be seen,
  But it's big as the sky at night . . .
I try to explain and it hurts my brain,
  But once I'm there, it's *right*.

There's a place I know inside myself,
  And it's neither big nor small,
And whenever I go, it feels as though
  I never left at all.

THE MOUSE THAT LIVES ON THE MOON

The mouse that lives on the moon
Plays the drum with a musical spoon—
    With a laugh like a loon
    He drums, night and noon,
To a musical, mousical tune.

And the cow plays the big bassoon
With her mouth like a macaroon—
    The cow on bassoon,
    While the mouse plays the spoon
In a musical, mousical,
Moo-sical, mouthical tune.

And softly in Saskatoon
A child hears the magical tune:
    The mouse on the moon
    With a silvery *BOOOM*,
    The mooing bassoon
    With a mystical tune,
    And a child who can croon
    To the faraway moon
In a musical, mousical,
Moo-sical, mouthical,
Mythical, mystical tune—
A tune with a moo and a spoon,
The tune of the mouse on the moon!

MY LIFE IN A SHOE

When I was a baby, I thought I was big—
I lived in a running shoe,
And I used to spread my raisin bread
With honey and buttercup dew.

And every day I went out to play
With the bear and the baby raccoon;
And every night, with a bright flashlight,
I swam in the pools of the moon.

Well, now I am three, and I'm big as can be,
And I act like a big kid too;
But part of me stays in the olden days
When I lived in a running shoe.

I'M NOT COMING OUT

Cover me over
With blankets in bed:
A sheet on my feet
And a quilt on my head,

A frown on my face
And a pout on my snout—
I'm sad, and I'm mad,
And I'm not coming out!

And I don't care if they tickle,
And I don't care if they tease;
I don't care if they beg me to
Until their bottoms freeze,

'Cause it isn't very funny
When a person feels this way,
And it won't be very funny
If a person runs away.

So I'm not coming out, and I'm *not* coming out,
And I'm NOT coming out—and then,
They'll tell me that they're sorry . . .
And I *might* come out again.

I'M NOT A NAUGHTY DAUGHTER

I'm not a naughty daughter.
I'm not a naughty son.
I'm not a naughty anything—
And now my story's done.

MARY ELLEN MONTAGUE

Mary Ellen Montague,
Won't you come to tea?

Mary Ellen Montague,
Don't you care for me?

If you will not heed my plea,
We must sadly part—

So Mary Ellen Montague,
Please return my heart.

LICKETY-SPLIT

Lickety-split and razzmatazz,
Lickety-split and dandy,
Lickety-split to the corner store
To buy a bag of candy.

One to give a hungry kid,
One to feed my family,
And one to stuff my famous face—
Eating a bag of candy!

ANTELOPE, A CANTALOUPE

Antelope, a cantaloupe,
I can't elope with you;
My poppa wants to come
And my momma does too.

Everybody wants to come,
And tell us what to do—
So antelope, a cantaloupe,
I can't elope with you!

COWARDY, COWARDY CUSTARD

Cowardy, cowardy custard,
Your mouth is made of mustard:
    You talk all day—
    Then you run away,
Cowardy, cowardy custard!

144

FOLLOW THAT WHALE

Follow that whale, Mister Snail.
Follow that whale, Mister Snail.
    Follow that whale
    And catch him by the tail,
And follow that whale, Mister Snail!

Follow that dog, Mrs Frog.
Follow that dog, Mrs Frog.
    Follow that dog
    Till he leaps along a log,
And follow that dog, Mrs Frog!

Follow that cat, Mister Rat.
Follow that cat, Mister Rat.
    Follow that cat
    'Cause she's acting like a brat—
And follow that cat, Mister Rat!

GUMBO STEW

Momma, don't let me chew that gumbo stew
Momma, don't let me chew that gumbo stew
   'Cause if I chew that gumbo stew
   You know I'm gonna bloat till I block the view—
Please momma, don't let me chew that gumbo stew.

Poppa, don't let me chomp them gumbo fries
Poppa, don't let me chomp them gumbo fries
   'Cause if I chomp them gumbo fries
   You know I'm gonna swell ten times my size—
Now poppa, don't let me chomp them gumbo fries.

Gramma, don't let me taste no gumbo tart
Gramma, don't let me taste no gumbo tart
   'Cause if I taste that gumbo tart
   You know my belly's gonna bust apart—
Gra-gra-gra-gramma, don't let me taste no gumbo tart!

BAPPY EARTHDAY!

There's a tangle in my tungle
    And I can't rock tight,
And I reel so feelie bungled
    That I set I book a light!

But I'm getting all invited,
    'Cause the farty will be pun
Which you graciously excited me
    To come to, sane or run.

So I gapped a little rift,
    Yes I lipped a riddle gaffe . . .
(When I sing "Bappy Earthday,"
    Don't let Benny Uddy laugh.)

BIG BAD BILLY

Big bad Billy
Had a button on his tum.

Big bad Billy
Said, "I'm gonna have some fun!"

Big bad Billy
Gave a tug, and then a shout—

And big bad Billy
Pulled his belly button out!

DIMPLETON THE SIMPLETON

Dimpleton the simpleton
    Went out to milk a cow.
Dimpleton the simpleton
    Could not remember how.

He pumped the tail, both high and low,
    To make the milk come out;
The cow went MOO, the bucket flew,
    And smacked him on the snout!

QUEEN FOR A DAY

Tina Corinna Christina the Third
Was queen in the land of Tra-La;
   She ruled for a day
   Till they put her away,
For sipping her tea with a straw.

CHICA

My girl friend's name is Chica,
She comes from Costa Rica.
She plays all day, in a very saucy way—
My cheeky Tica Chica.

AKI

My boy friend's name is Aki,
We snack on teriyaki.
With a quiver and a quack when I tickle his back—
My wacky, quacky Aki.

THE KITSILANO KID

Who's that stepping
    Down the street?
It's the Kitsilano Kid
    With the ricky-ticky beat.

Children leave the schoolyard,
    Coppers leave the beat,
For the Kitsilano Kid
    And the ricky-ticky beat.

People know he's near
    By the tickle in their feet—
It's the Kitsilano Kid
    With the ricky-ticky beat, *hey!*
The Kitsilano Kid
    With the ricky-ticky beat!

THE LOTTERY DREAM OF MISS PATRICIA PIG

When I am rich,
I shall live in a ditch.
And I'll wriggle and scratch
Whenever I itch.

SKINNY MARINKA DINKA

Skinny marinka dinka dine,
A puppy met a porcupine.
The puppy barked and ran away—
Skinny marinka dinka day!

CHICKADEE, FLY!

Chickadee, chickadee
Fly away;
Chickadee, chickadee
Do not stay;

Or you will be,
In no time flat,
A chickadee dinner
For a hungry cat!

POLLIWOGS

When polliwogs are paddling
    In the puddles in the park,
Y' know they don't much mind
    If it's light or dark.

They do the wibble-wobble
    As they shimmy in the pool—
Then they flip their little fannies,
    And they swim to school.

154

CHITTER-CHATTER-CHIPMUNK

Chitter-chatter-chipmunk,
    Fussing on a fence:
All you do is run around
    And get in arguments.

Acorns by the acre full,
    But all you do is scold—
Gather some, and bury some,
    Before the earth is cold.

DING, DONG

DING, DONG,
A short, sad song—
The cat's in a tizzy
'Cause her kittens are gone.

SNICK, SNACK

SNICK, SNACK,
A paddy-whack—
The cat's going crazy
'Cause her kittens came back!

THE BUTTERFLY

Butterfly,
    butterfly,
life's a
    dream;

all that we
    see,
and all that we
    seem,

here for a
    jiffy
and then
    goodbye—

butterfly,
    butterfly,
flutter
    on by.

I KNOW IT'S TIME

I know it's time
To say good night.
I know, it's time:
Turn out the light . . .

But I loved the one
With the princess proud,
And the one that made us
Laugh out loud;

I loved the one
About the bears,
And that other one,
Where the Daddy cares—

And sometimes I
Could nearly cry,
'Cause I feel so full
And I don't know why

As here on the bed
We ride up high,
And the story goes on,
And the night goes by,

And one day I'll
Be big, I guess,
And I'll have some kids,
And I'll love them best

And I'll tell them the stories
You told to me
(But I'll love you still,
And I'll bring you tea . . .)

And now it's time:
Turn out the light.
I love you—it's time—
It's time . . . *Good night*.

ROSE PETALS PINK

Rose petals pink,
Rose petals red,
Rose petals resting
On your sleepytime head.

(Funny little darling,
Snuggled into bed—
Rose petals dreaming
In your sleepytime head.)

SECRETS

Columbine is sweet
And sweet alyssum blooming—
Tell me who you love,
And I'll whisper what I'm dreaming.

Far as silver stars
In rippled darkness gleaming—
Tell me who you love,
And I'll whisper what I dream of.

Deep as hollow logs,
When phantom frogs are booming—
Tell me who you love,
And I'll whisper what I'm dreaming, dreaming of.

BY THE LIGHT OF THE MOON

The sky tonight
    Is a silvery spray:
It's such strange light
    I'm a world away

As I watch the trees
    And the buildings float
On the rockabye breeze . . .
    And the moon's a boat,

And the boat slips by
    In a dream of space,
And my heart rides high—
    I love this place!

A HOME LIKE A HICCUP

If I'd been born in a different place,
With a different body, a different face,
And different parents and kids to chase—
    I might have a home like a hiccup:

Like Minsk! or Omsk! or Tomsk! or Bratsk!
Like Orsk or Kansk! like Kirsk or Murmansk!
Or Lutsk, Irkutsk, Yakutsk, Zadonsk,
    Or even Pskov or Moskva!

But then again, on a different day
I might have been born a world away,
With brand-new friends and games to play—
    And a home like a waterfall whisper:

Like Asti, Firenze, Ferrara, Ravenna,
Like Rimini, Pisa, Carrara, Siena,
Like Napoli, Como, San Marco, San Pietro,
    Or Torre Maggiore, or Roma.

Now, those are places of great renown.
But after I'd studied them up and down,
I chose to be born in my own home town—
    So the name of *my* place is _____.

GOOF ON THE ROOF

Quick! quick! quickly!
Quiet as a mouse!
   There's a goof
   On the roof,
And he's eating up the house . . .

Slow, slow, slowly,
Drag him down again.
   There he goes
   Up your nose—
Now he's eating up your brain!

DOOBY, DOOBY

My friend is such a bore,
She bugs me more and more;
She's got this stupid rhyme—
And she says it all the time!

    'Cause she goes,
    Dooby, dooby, in your eye
    Dooby, dooby, punkin pie

    Dooby, dooby, in your hair
    Dooby, dooby, I don't care.

Now, for a little while,
That poem made me smile;
But now it's such a drag,
It makes me want to gag!

    'Cause she goes,
    Dooby, dooby, in your eye
    Dooby, dooby, punkin pie

    Dooby, dooby, in your hair
    Dooby, dooby, I don't care.

Each time I met that kid
I nearly flipped my lid—
Until I got the knack,
And made her stop her yack!

    'Cause I go,
    Dooby, dooby, in your eye
    Dooby, dooby, punkin pie

    Dooby, dooby, in your hair
    Dooby, dooby, I don't care.

LULU

My girl friend's name is Lulu,
She comes from Honolulu.
With an ice cream scoop, and a hula hoop—
My Honolulu Lulu.

JUMBO

My boy friend's name is Jumbo,
He came here from Colombo.
He's big as a house, but he's shy as a mouse—
My gentle giant, Jumbo.

SHAKE-'N'-BAKE A JELLY

If you want a jelly dinner
That's as tasty as can be,
You can shake-'n'-bake a jelly
With a special recipe.

First you bake it in the oven
In a jelly-baking pan;
Then you plop it on your belly
Just as fast as you can;

And your top shakes a little,
And your bottom shakes a lot,
And your middle gives a twiddle
Till your tummy's in a knot;

Then the jelly starts to wibble
On your jelly-belly-pot—
And you've shake-'n'-baked your jelly,
And you serve it, piping hot!

BETTY, BETTY

Betty, Betty,
Cook spaghetti,
Tie it in knots
With pink confetti,

Eat it with ketchup,
Eat it with cheese—
Eat it with gusto
If you please!

POPPING POPCORN

I pop popcorn,
You pop popcorn,
He pops—she pops—
We all pop popcorn!

Pop it in a pot, or
Pop it in a pan;
Pop it in the popper
Like the popcorn man!

HAMMY, THE ESCAPE HAMSTER

I had a little hamster,
And Hammy was his name,
And every time I locked him up
He ran away again.

I put him in a shoe-box,
But I didn't shut the lid;
He ran away that very day
Behind my bed and hid.

So when I caught old Hammykins,
I kept him in my shirt—
But grinning wide, he snuck outside
And woofled in the dirt.

Well then I cornered Hammy,
And I stuck him in a keg.
He took to flight that very night,
And went to Winnipeg.

And then I tried a cupboard
With a special lock and key.
Hammy didn't stick around,
He waltzed to Tennessee.

So then my bright idea was,
To plop him in a kettle.
The hamster hit the road again
For Popocatepetl.

And after that I caught the brat
And wedged him in a drawer—
He made a ladder out of socks
And split for Singapore.

Well, then I tried this iron cage
We bought for our canary.
But with a whoop he flew the coop
And crossed the Kalahari.

So then I put him on a raft,
And launched it in a pool—
The varmint did a cannonball
And swam to Istanbul!

And next a safe, inside a vault,
Inside a ten-ton barrow—
The dirty rascal steered the works
To Rio de Janeiro!

Till finally I sealed him
In a giant gas balloon:
Hammy set the gas alight,
And blasted to the moon!!

But now I've found the answer
And I'm much more satisfied;
Whenever Hammy runs away—
I trot along beside.

THE WATER-GO-ROUND

Oh, the sea makes the clouds,
   And the clouds make the rain,
And the rain rains down
   On the mighty mountain chain;

Then the silver rivers race
   To the green and easy plain—
Where they hurry, flurry, scurry
   Till they reach the sea again,

And the sea makes the clouds,
   And the clouds make the rain . . .

WILD!

Wild!—wild!—wild!
I am a human child.
The earth was here before we came
And *wild!—wild!—wild!*

Die!—die!—die!
The wild things say goodbye
Each time we take their homes away,
And *die!—die!—die!*

Do!—do!—do!
Before the earth is through,
We have to make it green again—
So *do!—do!—do!*

PETER PING AND PATRICK PONG

When Peter Ping met Patrick Pong
They stared like anything,
For Ping (in fact) looked more like Pong,
While Pong looked more like Ping.

The reason was, a nurse had changed
Their cribs, and got them wrong—
So no one knew, their whole lives through,
That Pong was Ping; Ping, Pong.

THE PIG IN PINK PYJAMAS

A pig in pink pyjamas
Went off to the balmy Bahamas—
    Where he sunned at night,
    For fear that the light
Would fade his pink pyjamas.

The pig in pink pyjamas
Came back from the balmy Bahamas—
    But his skin was bare,
    For the damp night air
Had rotted his pink pyjamas!

O pigs in pink pyjamas,
Beware of the balmy Bahamas—
    Where the sun's too bright,
    And the tropical night
Will rot your pink pyjamas,
    Oh-ho!
It will shrink, it will shrivel
And swinkle and swivel
    And rot your pink pyjamas!

DOWN IN PATAGONIA

Down in Patagonia
A walrus caught pneumonia,
From playing its trombonia
While swimming all alonia.

(So when in Patagonia
A walrus on its ownia
Should play the xylophonia,
To guard against pneumonia.)

THE MOTORCYCLE DRIVER

A motorcycle driver drove
    Along a winding road;
He wore a leather jacket,
    And he met a warty toad.

The driver sighed, "I'd like to snooze
    All day beside the road."
"I'd like to drive a big black motor-
    Cycle," cried the toad.

And so the driver settled down
    Beside the winding road.
And off the motorcycle roared,
    Driven by—*the toad!*

FOG LIFTING

In Stewiacke and Mushaboom
I didn't see a thing;
At Musquodoboit Harbour, I could
Hear the foghorn sing;

At Ecum Secum I discovered
Colours in the sea—
And I learned to look at living things
In Shubenacadie.

THE FIB

I found the fib on Friday
    In a pile of styrofoam.
It looked so cute and cuddly
    I just had to bring it home.
        It was a teeny, tiny fib,
          It's true—
        Till the darn thing grew!

Next morning I was puzzled,
    For the fib was getting fat;
It ate a dozen doughnuts
    And it tried to eat the cat.
        It was a bratty little fib
        So I stuck it in the crib,
          It's true—
        But the darn thing grew!

Next day at five, the fib revived
  And made a dreadful din:
It shinnied down a sheet it found
  And kicked the T.V. in.
    It was a healthy, growing fib
    And it didn't like the crib
    So I dressed it in a bib,
      It's true—
    But then the darn thing grew!

Well, day by day the fib just lay
  And slurped its fuzzy fur.
And night by night, in the pale moonlight
  It munched the furniture.
    It was a whopping giant fib
    And it gobbled up the crib
    And it wouldn't wear a bib
    And its laugh was loud and glib
      It's true—
    And still the darn thing grew!

The final morning, when I woke,
  The fib was in my room.
Its fibby lips began to twitch;
  I knew I faced my doom.
    Then I was swallowed by the fib,
    Landing on the chewed-up crib,
    Nearly smothered by the bib
    In the laughter loud and glib
    As it roared of Fibbers' Lib,
      It's true—
    While on and on, and on and on
    Until the end of time shall dawn—
      The darn fib grew!

JENNY THE JUVENILE JUGGLER

Jenny had hoops she could sling in the air
And she brought them along to the Summerhill Fair.
And a man from the carnival sideshow was there,
Who declared that he needed a juggler.

    And it's,
        Oops! Jenny, whoops! Jenny,
        Swing along your hoops, Jenny,
        Spin a little pattern as you go;
    Because it's
        Oops! Jenny's hoops! Jenny,
        Sling a loop-the-loop, Jenny,
        Whoops! Jenny, oops! Jenny, O!

Well the man was astonished at how the hoops flew,
And he said, "It's amazing what some kids can do!"
And now in the carnival, Act Number Two
Is Jenny the Juvenile Juggler.

    And it's,
        Oops! Jenny, whoops! Jenny,
        Swing along your hoops, Jenny,
        Spin a little pattern as you go;
    Because it's
        Oops! Jenny's hoops! Jenny,
        Sling a loop-the-loop, Jenny,
        Whoops! Jenny, oops! Jenny, O!

MRS MITCHELL'S UNDERWEAR

Mrs Mitchell's underwear
    Is dancing on the line;
Mrs Mitchell's underwear
    Has never looked so fine.

Mrs Mitchell hates to dance—
    She says it's not refined,
But Mrs Mitchell's underwear
    Is prancing on the line.

With a polka-dotted polka
    And a tangled tango too,
Mrs Mitchell's underwear
    Is like a frilly zoo!

DOH-SI-DOH

Don't be lazy,
    Don't be late—
Jump right over
    The garden gate

Bring your grampa
    Bring your gran
Pile them into
    The old sedan

And it's one for lights
    And two for luck
As we nearly collide
    With the pick-up truck!

Now here's the fiddler
    Big and fat
Mopping his brow
    With an old felt hat

And here's the caller
    Short and sweet
Trim in the middle
    And quick on her feet

So upsy-daisy
    Don't be lazy
Allemande left
    Till it drives you crazy

Swing with Peter
    Swing with Paul
Swing with the boy
    Who's the best in the hall.

And it's tickle my fancy!
    Tickle my tum!
Tickle my ribs
    Till I beat like a drum!

178

Now don't be rude
    And don't be rowdy
Tell your lovin'
    Partner "Howdy!"

When he makes
    A bow, by heck,
Grab him round
    His lovin' neck

Swing him quick
    Across the floor—
Pitch him smartly
    Out the door!

And you be candy
    I'll be gum
As we grand-change-all
    Into kingdom come . . .

But now the doh-
    Si-dohs are through;
Back in the truck,
    And be
                home . . .
                    by . . .
                        two.

LUCY GO LIGHTLY

Lucy go lightly
    Wherever you go,
Light as a lark
    From your head to your toe;

In slippers you float
    And in sandals you flow—
So Lucy, go lightly
    Wherever you go.

NIGHT SONG

The golden sun
    Has set for good
On every street
    In the neighbourhood.

Now through the dark
    And dusky deep
The swallows flutter
    Home to sleep,

And all my friends
    Have snuggled in
To where the sleepy
    Times begin.

Soon other children
    Far away,
From Borneo
    To Bristol Bay,

Will say good night
    The way I do,
And dream of far-off
    Places too—

As night comes snuggling
    Soft and curled,
Around the block,
    Around the world.